These are my parents. I have known them my whole life.

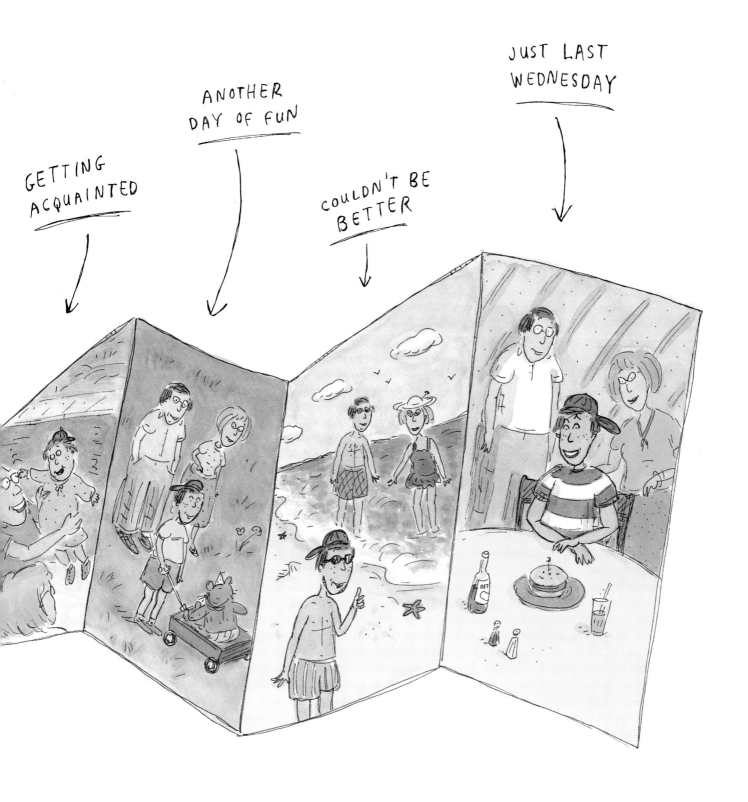

GETTING ACQUAINTED

ANOTHER DAY OF FUN

COULDN'T BE BETTER

JUST LAST WEDNESDAY

And now . . .

This is Miss Peck. She is in charge of kissing Aunt Winnie,

which is something I would rather not do.

1000 feet
If laid end to end, would reach Moon

750 feet
Would fill the Grand Canyon

500 feet
Entire long underwear supply of France

250 feet
Heavier than 200 elephants

Speaking of Aunt Winnie, every winter she sends me another pair of long underwear. Do you know who sends Aunt Winnie a thank-you note?

Monsieur Monsieur, my Personal Letter Writer.

Feather Bella, my Costume-ologist, irons my Halloween costume
every morning so I can wear it for the millionth day in a row.

Mozart practices my piano lessons.

My Room Crew works on toys, especially fixing them. I break them myself.

Say hello to Herr Von Where, my Thing Finder. The day Herr Von Where lost his glasses, I was in big trouble.

There's the Homework Helper. Ask him anything.

The Lima Bean Man knows how to eat all the lima beans off my plate without crying or making a face. He also takes care of Brussels sprouts, squash, and radishes in salad.

Delores De-cruster cuts the crust off my bread.

Whenever I am in the mood for birthday cake, Old Stu has another birthday. Old Stu has worked for me only two years, but already he is over 8,392 years old.

I do not like green candy of any kind, and thanks to the Candy Sorter and Remover, I never have to worry.

When I am sick from eating too much non-green candy,

I. M. Better swallows my pink medicine.

# Last Place Larry is really bad at

checkers

miniature golf

splashing contests

rock throwing

catch

rummy

bowling

Dizzy Dizzy Dog

When I crack a joke, my Laughers always laugh.

Mr. Up helps on the hills.

Sir Yes, But is my Explainer.

But there are some things that even Sir Yes, But cannot explain. . . .

Luckily Mrs. Wrong is happy to sit in the time-out chair for me.

H$_2$O Flo makes sure I always have a straw.

Sometimes I am not in the mood for a bath, so Admiral B. fills in.

Not that I'm afraid, but before I go to bed,
the Inspector checks for:

sharks
monsters
anti-matter
other dimensions
lockjaw
invisible alien warriors

patches of quicksand
unauthorized personnel
zombies
oil spills
strangers
radioactive lint

poltergeists
dust devils
sinkholes
wind spouts
electricity leaking
from sockets

After the Inspector says my room is clean, I take the gum out of my mouth and hand it over to the Gum Guy, who saves it all night long.

And when it is time for bed, the Dream Team does that for me,

while I wonder how I will get through tomorrow...

...on my staff's day off!

Meet My Staff

Text copyright © 1998 by Patricia Marx

Illustrations copyright © 1998 by Roz Chast

Printed in the U.S.A. All rights reserved.

---

Library of Congress Cataloging-in-Publication Data

Marx, Patricia (Patricia A.)

Meet my staff / by Patricia Marx ; illustrated by Roz Chast.

p.        cm.

"Joanna Cotler Books."

Summary: Young Walter introduces his imaginary "staff" of toy-fixers, piano practicers,

sandwich de-crusters, and beast inspectors.

ISBN 0-06-027484-0.

[1. Imagination–Fiction.]    I. Chast, Roz, ill.    II. Title.

PZ7.M36823Me    1998                                        96-37678

[E]–dc21                                                          CIP

AC

---

1  2  3  4  5  6  7  8  9  10

First Edition


Visit us on the World Wide Web!

http://www.harperchildrens.com

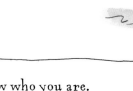

To our OWN staff—you know who you are.

P.M. and R.C.

1,2,3: Walter's Banner Boys • 4: Miss Peck • 5: Monsieur Monsieur • 6: Feather Bella • 7: Mozart • 8,9: Room Crew •
10: Herr Von Where • 11: Homework Helper • 12: Lima Bean Man • 13: Delores De-cruster • 14: Old Stu •